The Book of a Runner

Pablo Lazo

 New Generation Publishing

"the path of practice:
where will be
my final resting place?"

Old Japanese Haiku.

Torreon, Coahuila, Mexico, March 10, 1996

It's hot and humid and it is only 6am. I have my gear with me. I go straight into the changing area. A good dozen elite runners are there already. Some other people, non runners, are there already. It's early for them to be there, even with the cups of coffee and some food. The sun hasn't come out yet but you can feel that it will be a warm day.

The start line is just across the main gate of the milk factory that sponsors the race. Some of the cars belonging to other runners were allowed into the factory so as to be closer to the changing and warm up areas. A few familiar faces that I recognize are close by, but most people I don't know. Good runners? Bad runners, or marathon debutants? I don't know. The factory has a huge courtyard where runners are stretching, warming up or queuing up for the toilets. It is still too early to say if this is a massive event or just a few hundred runners.

I brought two pairs of running shoes; weather depending, I may use the flat, light old *Nike* if it is hot and humidity could increase; or, as it seems, I might use the heavier and more supportive *Asics 2021*. They might just work better on the asphalt if the temperature is not too high.

I pick up my number and racing chip near the main gate. 'Elite runners' says a big red banner above. Fidel and Alcala already have their numbers and they are with other runners.

'Ready to go fast?' asks Fidel.

'I don't know yet, will see'

'Take it easy on the first part, it's downhill..'

'Yeah, yeah'

Near where I'm stretching, another runner wearing a vest that I recognize, Viveros running club, is stretching and tightening his laces. His number is also a two digit one, which means he's running in the elite race as well. We exchange minor greetings, as I pass by and I see he has the same light *Nike* shoes I do and he's going to run with them. The course has some parts with uneven surfaces; a very light shoe could be dreadful on those surfaces. I know this because I have jogged some parts of the course.

Last few sips from my bottle of water with special energy liquid. I go for an easy warm up with Fidel, he wants to win this race; I want to qualify for the world university games. Two different races at the same time, this is the paradoxical beauty of running.

The marathon of LALA is the most important in the northern region of Mexico. The 42.195 km course covers three cities which are close by: Torreon, Gomez-Palacio and Laguna. The course is very flat and fast with a few minor hills, and a section called the viaduct that has about 5 flyovers to go through. It normally holds the national championship, the trial race for the Olympic national team and that's why it is the best marathon of the year in Mexico.

The guy from Viveros is at the front line doing some strides. He's wearing a band in his head and glasses so I can't see his eyes. Is he looking at me? Does he know me? He is pretending not to look at anybody but I'm sure he is also nervous. I put my sugar gummy bear in my short pocket: two halves, one for each 21 km. I won't drink any special drinks through the course, only water and the gummy bears.

There are some really fast pacers already at the front, Pitayo, Quintanilla and Barrios I recognize. Surely they are rabbits, aren't they? I jog a bit more; the start is on a long straight, wide enough so there should be no crowding problems. After about 2km there is a left turn into the city centre, I should be already in pace and in a group by then, I think. There is an ad of "Crema Nivea" on the wall at that point, I must remember this mark.

I jog back to the start line, get in the left side, second row. Fidel is in front with his Fila sponsor vest.

'Look at the clouds, they will help to keep it cool' he says.

'Yeah, but still it's quite humid and there are some sections with pebbles', I say.

'Remember to drink water every 5km, in small sips, it's almost nothing but it will help'.

'I'll do' I reply calmly.

'Did you finally decide to wear the *Asics*?'

Fidel is tall and thin, he has the virtue of only wearing very light shoes, and he gives the impression of going really fast.

German Silva, a two-time winner of the New York City marathon, used to drink only water through the race, even on very hot and humid conditions. Only on the final 7 kilometers he would get one of his gummy bears and have it. Andres Espinosa, his former training buddy, saw him do this for 5 or 6 years until he finally asked him why. Silva, a proper gentleman explained: A good runner knows exactly when the body needs something more than water. You try to drink some isotonic fluids early in the race and your body won't take it, you will suffer stomach cramps and vomiting; if you leave it for very late, it's wasted, you're tired long before. Otherwise ask the great Haile Gebrselassie what it feels like to run only with water. He probably lost the 2002 London Marathon for this reason.

Normally, your energy is depleted after 32 kilometers. So, I learned to get the signal and I would shift to the glucose only at the very right moment. The chances of getting it too late were slim. I would take my chance.

Garrido is from Veracruz just like Silva. He claims to have run against him more times than he can remember. He never beat him as he is on a completely different level than Silva; also because Silva is good and very aggressive, according to Garrido. But sometimes a really good runner is someone who knows how to be cautious and patient.

I usually finish before Garrido but he is faster on shorter distances, I need to be aware of this if we end up running together until the last few meters – I say to myself.

Garrido is only legs and body. Among runners he is known as "the donkey" The fact is, he is not very clever. Human beings are made of two parts: mind and body. Of the two, a runner needs the mind to be sharp at racing. This mind has, of course, resources: legs and lungs –both of which should be calibrated well in advance, but it doesn't mean too much on the day of the race. What Silva normally has is faith and luck.

Jose Isidro Rico used to train only on hard courses and at very high altitude near his home town. The Faibrasse brothers used to have twenty miles on their legs every day training for a marathon they would jog to and back from work in the City of London at least nine months before the race. Leonard Riley always wears the oldest racers he has –and during a shivering cold and muddy cross country race I have seen him pouring cold water on his spikes to mold them and avoid blisters. Jose Reyes never finished without collapsing at the finish line. And the list is long.

If they wouldn't have let Silva take his special drink, at the very precise moment he needed it, he would never have won the New York City marathon.

I do the last few strides from the start line, chew half of a gummy bear and put the other half under my tongue. I will need that energy later, I say to myself.

All the big names are already at the start line. Three minutes to the start.

'Feeling ok?' A girl behind me asks.

'It's kind of difficult to say before I get going. And you?'

She smiles with irony and starts telling me how good she felt the last couple of weeks. All runners have an air of irony before the race, anyway. As if they are afraid to accept the fact that no one is going to judge you before the race. Once I heard a guy in the changing room say: 'I've been training to avoid excuses on race days'. There was silence and serious faces, and the guy probably was afraid his statement was taken seriously as a premonition of how fit he was.

The car with the clock, the race director and the press is a hundred meters ahead of us. I will loose sight of the clock very quickly. The man on the start line stands up and takes the megaphone. He tells the crowd this year the marathon of La Laguna hosts the national championship; he also explains how the course is a fast and flat covering three cities. He tells us that there is a prize for the course record. Aaron is standing in front of

9

me. We greet each other. I point to the car. 'Can you break the record today?'

Smiling he replies: 'with all the other good guys around I would rather not'.

Aaron is my regular training buddy. The two of us have studied this course together and he has run part of this course before as a half marathon. We chose to come and try this one. But he's in the same club as Fidel and, although the race is an individual affair, team strategy does play an important role in the early stages.

I'm standing behind the front row. It doesn't matter and it's warmer with lots of runner around, some of them still have their space blanket on top. This is by far the best strategy: not to be seen in the front line, but also to be close enough to the start so that no time is wasted.

I figured this out a while ago, on my 50th race. It was my first serious half marathon in Monterrey. It was a difficult hilly course where standing at the front row made no difference. We ran at turtle-like pace for the first few kilometers through the centre of the city. A big group of twenty five runners, packed like in a tuna can, without space, different, I thought.

On that occasion, as soon as we left the centre, the leading car ahead accelerated and the full pack stretched in front of me. Before I could react, the first big incline was there, and within a hundred meters, a gap was created between the leading pack and the chasers. My legs were hurting, the long incline had made me feel tired, and before the top I was at the back of the chasing pack, with no sight of the car. That lasted for a few minutes. Through the next flat section, I passed no one, no one passed me; the wind was behind and that helped me to come back to the back of the pack. Just when I was starting to feel the pace ease down, the next big incline came. At the top, a long straight section gave me some clues: some ten runners ahead, a huge gap, ten or so more runners ahead. The group had exploded causing big damage. With twenty minutes or so and five kilometers to go, the race was over. I was in the top fifty in a race I could have finished in the top ten.

As in many situations in life, racing tactics require patience; it seems a Mexican amateur normally has to learn like this.

Suddenly I feel the need to go to the toilet; there is no time, a local orchestra is playing the national Mexican anthem, all the runners around me make the flag stand (are standing at attention), elbows widening making the salute; when it's over, we're gone. Most of the runners around me have their hands on the stop-watch ready to start. I've been anticipating this moment for the last three months.

Kilometer 1

Spectators are packed for the first few meters on both sides of the road. They clap and shout "suerte, vamos, duro muchachos". A few pushes while the necessary space is made to really start running; someone shouts, "Watch the kicks". There it is: the first complaint we hear, I say to myself.

To the left, there is the old city centre of Torreon, with its old wood constructions and low buildings peeping in the horizon nearby. We will pass through this area later on, but from here it looks like an old industrial town whose time has long gone.

11

The pace of the leaders starts to pick up although I still see the car with the clock and the press with their huge tele-lens. I'm behind in the second group, some people around me I recognize, they are 2 hours thirty or so runners and they are older than I am, they know their best bet is to go slow now. Still, the leaders are in sight, my legs feel fine and the lungs even better. I started to run when I was 23 years old; too late for athletics but not for distance running.

After one kilometer, a compact guy shoots off, as in a sprint, and leaves a gap of ten meters in front of us. He's Blas Perez, he doesn't stand a chance in hell but he prefers to have his two minutes of glory and be remembered as the stupid guy who sprinted five kilometers in a marathon. We will catch him soon; he'll be blown up by then and won't be able to keep up.

Kilometer 2

His gap opens more, almost one hundred meters; he's doesn't have the typical runner complexity and his style is dreadful (he twists his head from one side to another, even more pronounced than the great Paula Radcliff). He seems to be overweight but he has some speed. The group where I'm in could not care less. We are almost at the city limits, few people watching, some kids and a dog are playing on the footpath and signs of poverty in the distance, but the road swiftly turns and that scene disappears. Still two and a half hours to go.

I look down to my bib number: 63. The pins are ok and my vest is still dry and I look down to my legs and try to catch a glimpse of my socks and laces – hoping that they will stand for the whole race. Suddenly I imagine a lace going loose and stopping to tighten it again – that would be a disaster, I think.

Kilometer 3

Someone says something to me, he's just behind, and it's Aaron. "The pace is slow" he says, "gear up" and he just passes me and gets in front. We're supposed to run together and pace each other, but he is gearing up too early. I have to tell this to Fidel, it's way out of line.

The pace is fine. The real race hasn't started. This group will probably stay together until the 25 km mark or thereabouts, and then we'll see. I'm waiting for that moment to start just like I want to finish when I'm at that point.

Some runners are chatty and come close by and start talking. I don't have a problem with that, but the conversation turns daft. Someone said to me once "if you can chat then you're not racing". It seems to me that these guys are going too slowly. Maybe they are only doing 21 kilometers and are pacing somebody else. Soon the chat will be over, I have never seen someone finish a race chatting but of course, you can do whatever you want on the race, even ask a fellow runner to give you his drink if you miss the drinking station or, as I saw it once, just grab a sponge from their hands.

I remain inside the group. My pace is calculated but effortless, probably because I just get along with the pace of the pack and it seems to me an easy jog. A row of trees appears on one side of the road. This is nice, I say in a low voice. I think we might be approaching the second city this race goes through. The guy at the front looks as if he's having a hard time but his pace is barely different from mine. The pack is working for me.

The marathon is one of the few road distances that allows both runners with speed and those with strong stamina and pace; all this sometimes combined with team strategies. Why? Because the race is based on a strong mind and body, and it's impossible for both types of runners or teams to prevent some things from happening. The Kenyans are widely recognized to have won many championships with the help of a team strategy and having the right runner in the right place. But still the runner who wins normally is the one who has the strongest mind of all on the day, and that is something unpredictable.

Until we don't see a group of Kenyans finishing a marathon together and handshaking, things will remain the same.

Having said that, the equalizing effect of running on the back of another runner is not too big. I would dare to accept that Tergat could very easily escape from the leading pack when he broke the half marathon record. I would also dare to assert that I could have paced Tergat slower when he did 59min. 19sec. but I could not have gone beyond 19 kilometers with that time. Not even with Tergat pushing my back saying "come on Lazo!!"

Kilometer 4

A small band is playing a Beatles song in spanglish. I pick up the lyrics and think of the Great North Run. I'm sure they have that as well. The trees are still there as we pass a couple of silly runners who started at the front and weren't fit enough. The group stays compact and the pace stills feel slow. At this point a very annoying thought comes to me: how about doing a half marathon today and try to get a PB? This is not the distance for today. Crazy idea and I forget it.

The real half marathon record is held by the great Ethiopian Haile Gebrselassie at 59min. 07sec. It was done at the perfect race, in a flat and fast course with perfect weather and with a motorbike going exactly at the speed needed.

An athletic history: New York City Marathon, 1981

A very level race was predicted between two great runners, and there was talk about the equalizing effect of running together and pushing each other.

On a windy morning, just after 20 kilometers, Alberto Salazar of the United States made a surge and left the leading pack static. Gomez, one of the other contenders, was finished. Salazar went on to conquer the first of his double wins. For the second part of the race, over the hilly parts of the course in Central Park, the favorite remained in front of the leading group, alone, finally arriving at the Tavern on the Green with a lead of 2 minutes 39 seconds.

That kind of thing doesn't happen.

I have seen photos of Salazar during that escape. Long strides, relaxed arms floating beside the chest, a flying Cuban goes by. Behind him, the chasers are working together, packed to protect themselves from the tailwind, pushing each other up every hill, trying to catch up: Jones, Gomez, Cabanillas, Sandoval and Toivola. The pursuit continues for more than an hour without success. Everybody in the press truck was able to see, in the distance, the figure of the enlightened man stretching along Fifth Avenue as if to show, with every stride, how the wind was lifting him.

When Salazar crossed the line in a course record of 2hs 8min 13sec, he passed his hand over his head and said he surged because he felt others were just going to do it. When he realized the big gap he made, with the long drag on Second Avenue in front of him, he decided to keep pushing it. " … guess I just ran very fast today".

16

No other escape like the 1981 NYC marathon has ever been seen again. Seeing Salazar that year, you could tell that it was the end of the age of innocence in the marathon. But his career didn't last long. He paid the price for pushing to the limit at every race.

Kilometer 5

The arrival to Gomez-Palacio, Durango, is indicated by a change in the topography. A flat section with trees on one side of the road which has been with us for almost two kilometers now; stay on the shade I think. Aaron is nowhere in sight. The guy leading the group turns his head back and shouts: "It's going to be hot today".

Just getting into the town, Samuel makes a surge. Silly, it's too early. In his dark vest he smoothly strides away from us. He has stamina and is a good distance runner; so why doesn't he just stay and run with us? I could also make the surges as he does if I wanted to. "Lazo made the greatest sacrifices of all, he heard the cheering of the crowd at the beginning, and then he dropped out and had another DNF".

Nobody reacts to Samuel's surge. Gustavo, one of the best in the group and a favorite to finish in the top ten, comes up and runs by my side. His red vest looks impeccable and I can see he has a cap in his short −for later, I think. I quickly check his face, he is talking but I can't understand a word, but I take it he is also thinking "there goes Samuel, a moron".

Then something amazing happens: I start to accelerate and get a few meters away from the group. Like a youngster on his first race. I stretch my arms, every stride is wider, and I'm breathing deep, air getting right into my lungs. I'm getting closer to the back of Samuel and I hear the rest of the group saying, "let it go, let it go". It seems like a long pause, my eyes are fixed on a lady crossing a few meters in front of us, and suddenly I'm running along Samuel, I caught him.

Now he seems not to recognize me, his stride and style is not the best. His arms and legs are all over the place; I push and go in front of him.

Today the routine will not happen. It will be a different day. This push is decisive and I'll go and pass Fidel like a piece of fluff, destroy the rest of the group in the first steep uphill and I'll run solo the final seven kilometers, my place among the top ten will be talked about for years to come.

I feel the burning pain that defines the distinction between attack and rhythm. I must be crazy, if they leave me alone I'll just be amused at my own enthusiasm and imaginary strength. Let Lazo go like a rabbit. All they have to do is stay a few meters behind until I fall apart and start to go backwards.

Samuel takes over again. I glace back to see who is coming; the group is just behind us. Aaron's glasses stand out in front and just hiding behind is Gustavo in his yellow vest of Viveros club. Samuel makes a sign with his hand accusingly and slows his pace.

Kilometer 6

Again someone surges and the pace picks up. Then the pace slowly calms down. The tailwind kind of helps to feel the relief of the not-so-hot breeze; now that I have time to think again, it occurs to me that there was nothing crazy about my surge that early. How did I forget? I normally start the first few kilometers quite brisk to put the blood vessels in alert. The group packs together as the pace is even slower. Some guys relax their arms and others seem to look around as if to enjoy the landscape. Samuel is about 50 meters away now. Was he expecting us to catch up with him?

Strong and with firm stride, like a tank, Aaron pulls away from the group once more. He glances and makes a sign with his hand and then accelerates a bit more followed by a youngster in green and yellow vest from Marina. He looks somewhat familiar.

We don't know if we will see Aaron again but there is this other guy from Marina, so now there are two runners in front, and Samuel, who can always can go and make a surge. I don't have a rabbit to control the pace, not like Gustavo. My club is weak. I only have a sort of secret pact with Gerardo, but Gerardo is a contender as well so he'd rather save his energy for later.

It's always too early, Frank Horwill used to say: 'Always attack as late as you can, but before others do.'

In fact there is no need to worry. In this race there are at least a couple of strong rival clubs: Rodolfo Gomez and Venados. The former has Pitayo, the always reliable Paredes, who came second to Silva in the great wrong turn in New York in 1994 and Bautista. The latter has Gustavo, Samuel and Fidel. If they don't take the initiative, then so be it.

The calm in the group continues. Ahead I can still see the guy from Marina and Aaron getting on one side of the road to get some water. Soon they will be with the leading pack. A motorcycle with a camera man passes by and shouts something to the guy at the front of the pack. I only read on his lips the word 'meters.'

Kilometer 7

The LALA marathon exits Gomez Palacio and enters the state of Coahuila with applauses from the spectators. The landscape changes dramatically: all of a sudden we are in a rural environment. A leading pack of six runners is being chased by a pack of twelve almost a minute behind.

Suddenly there is another surge by three runners in the group, one of them with a Venados vest. They must have been preparing this assault but it's still too early – is this some kind of team tactics? I ask myself. The rest of the group ignores this. The pace actually seems to drop. This is serious: Venados now has a runner in front as well and Fidel is one of the best runners around. I see his long strides and calm arms sweep by. I move to the front of the pack, now we're down to nine and I want to pick up the pace a little. If the rest would help now, we'd have those three back just like that. Hey, here is Samuel again. But once I have waved at him a few times, I notice that we're the only ones willing to take our pull. I look back, find Vicente stuck behind me, I blink my eyes and he does the same. He knows I'm asking for some help here but no answer. Lazy.

What am I supposed to do? The pack is a prison. I slow down, Vicente slows down, Samuel waits for somebody to run side by side in vain and looks at me like he wants to put me on a shelf. The group is compact and at some point hands are upfront to stop hitting somebody's back. 'Hey, are you guys going to race or shall we call it a day now?' Nobody stops but I slow down even more and sit at the back of the group.

Aldrete surges and goes away gently; we pass through a water station. There is no way out of this; I mustn't loose my patience. Nora-Leticia –the leading girl who was sitting at the back all this time also surges. This is better. To my surprise, everybody else lets her go. Within the next two kilometers they are with Aaron and the guy from Marina.

Kilometer 8

Sometimes running is a bit boring and can even seem pointless. This is the normal time in a race to think that, I recall this happening last time too. So why do a marathon again? Why are you racing against time? Because it's natural to go fast, replied the sprinter.

We've just gone over a flyover, one of the few inclines on this course. As we come down we make a sharp turn left and we are back into Torreon, running along a big river on a long straight; through the bend the group can get a sense of the trail of runners behind us, like a very long snake of bright colors, changing in shape and form as the eye stretches as far as possible. This occurs in just three seconds but feels very long. Up in front, I can still see the car lights of the leading pack. This is the industrial part of the city; a no-go area for the tourist and definitely an area where no runner would like to drop-out, but an ideal place to take a pee.

I estimate about fifteen runners ahead of us. I mustn't loose concentration; my race is with the people of this group. We are racing to qualify for the big race. Vicente, Samuel, Jose and Aaron are all on my group.

Samuel is the strongest of them. There are also four women: a blond one, from Britain they say, two Mexicans and a Kenyan. I think it would be nice to beat all the ladies. I have never done it before.

Every once in a while a spectator on the road lets us know how we are placed or that we're doing well. A man shouts: 'third group, top twenty places are in sight'. He probably thinks racing is about placing and that we are almost there.

I run alongside Vicente for the next kilometer or so. He is concentrated on the road. He relaxes his arms and I hear his breath, easy, calm, barely any sweat on his face. I look again at him, but he kind of ignores me. I know what he is thinking; I'm in this third group of youngsters but I'm one of the pre-race favorites. He is old now, his best days are gone and as soon as the surges start after the half way point he will struggle. Nevertheless his white hair inspires respect. Hell knows what tricky things he can pull together. And he is still an old fox. I have run against veterans and they always do the same. Start slow but in the end they pick up the pace and end one, two, five and ten minutes ahead of me. The worst day to realize you're racing against them is on race day.

My athletic history
November 1994

Where is the Verrazano Bridge? How to get there, why go there? Only one reason: to start running the New York City marathon.

This was the first time I experienced what cows and the sheep may well feel when they are directed through fences and narrow paths to "stables": only to wait for the final call, nerves on end and wanting to pee on a cold and wet November morning.

Almost ten years later, this sheep-like feeling, or should we say, shipping process is a general rule in every mass demonstration, athletic event, ecological rally or shopping day at Oxford Street during Christmas.

I was in the "under 3:00 hrs" corral. This meant a lot to me but everybody in there seemed to be better prepared than me. There was one guy in the corner, lying almost horizontally, covered by a space blanket. It was the first time I saw one of those people who seem to be almost levitating before the race. I approached him and asked how long we were going to be held there. 'The same as last year' he replied. 'But this is much more comfortable than if you are in the 4:00 hrs corral', he added. He turned out to be one of those freaks who have run all twenty five New York City marathons so far.

I walked back to the narrow corner of the 'corral' and waited patiently. There was a gloomy grey sky and I was just remembering things about the course: 'wait until the bridge into Manhattan and the turn into Second Avenue, that's when the real race starts' I said loudly to myself. I looked around, what on earth are they thinking? Nobody seemed to be looking. I was only worried about the rain, yes, simple as that. My trainers, dirty and heavy enough already were not ideal for this forecast. Anyway it was too late. For me, running was about challenging the weather.

Kilometre 9

A little band dressed like clowns is playing music: "...and we are the champions" I can hear loudly. What does Queen have to do with a marathon? A youngster besides the band shouts: "the leaders are 3 min ahead, run faster; this part of the course is flat". Aaron pulls to the side of the road where the youngster is and stares at him just as we pass by, the boy shuts up and we regroup in the centre of the road. Now the serious running will start. Someone said to me once that in a marathon you better think like it's three 12km races. Your mind can do that and the trick of concentrating on the first 12km and so on. It is your body which doesn't know how to do the trick. In 3 kilometres the first of three mini races will be over, I repeat to myself.

Every new kilometre is closer to the halfway point: there the comeback into Torreon will start and with that, the series of flyovers, eight in total if I remember well. That's where the race will be decided. The group is compact; the blond girl is running alongside me. She has a short stride but she's strong.

The last kilometre before entering the long straight and very boring section of the course is ahead. Few spectators on the course now, another ideal place to stop for the loo if necessary, I think as we pass a couple of street dogs laying below a tree on the side of the road, and further away there is a horse calmly eating his breakfast. One of the dogs lifts his head slowly to see what is going on. Are dogs clever enough to distinguish a slow runner from a fast one?

Suddenly I see the second pack of runners ahead.

That must be them! A few dots spread along the tarmac with the lights of one of the motorcycles blinking and the clock in light green. A slight feeling of indiscretion: like glimpsing over the shoulder of a friend to look at a naked girl. A girl I like but have never laid my hands on. I relax my legs and look around as I feel in a very confident state of mind where nothing seems impossible.

Kilometre 10

The first double digit km mark is represented by a big *Lucozade* air balloon standing on one side of the road and the strip on the pavement to record the split times. A big digital clock says: 33:21 for the first ten kilometres. Right on schedule for the 2hs:26mins qualifying time. We make a right turn and there is the long straight road. The group spreads a bit at the turn; Vicente and the blond girl pull to the side to grab their bottles at the drinking station. Hers is bright blue and yellow with a clear mark. Is this some kind of lucky amulet that elite runners bring to every race?

As I try to control my breath, a song comes to my mind and I start repeating the chorus line. This has worked in other races where the segments of the courses are boring. Your mind goes off with the lyrics and seems to enjoy more the minutes rolling over to let the time and the kilometres go by. I cannot think of a half marathon or a marathon in which you can't recall what was in your mind for at least a couple of kilometres. Good, your brain helps to compress the notion of time.

I feel someone hitting my hand; it is Vicente who is very close to my back. I turn and stare at him as I wave to indicate I need space here! He seems to not care. He is trying to hold on to this pace.

Kilometre 11

A sign: TORREON, Acceso Norte. At the long straight I see some guys making a surge. Everybody is nervous now, in the next five-kilometre split this group can come apart, some of the runners haven't run this far at this pace. And also the temperature will soon be rising. I can see the newspaper report: "youngsters paying the price of going too quick too early".

I have dropped back a little; I'm in the middle of the group. Gustavo surges but does it gently, it doesn't work; he turns around and slows down, curses and exchanges something with Vicente that I can't figure out. Vicente is the type of running buddy you don't really want to run with. He is annoying in every respect and he seems not to realize this. All the twelve runners in front of me now, the road looks full. I go and run along Aaron, a fine, lean running machine.

Some of the worst gaps occur when the pace is picked up on a long but constant pace surge. My eyes are wide open and alert for any change of pace. I panic that they're going to create a gap ahead of me; I still haven't got the right breathing rhythm. I touch the calf of a leg in front; someone shouts something, nothing else happens.

A motorcycle with a cameraman just reaches the group. I don't pay attention but they seem to be taking some short shots of us. All of a sudden they speed up and are gone. It would have been nice to have the company of the camera for a bit longer. Two runners make a huge surge and are gone. In 100 meters they have opened a gap of 20 meters. Do they believe they can go with the bike? They go running out of my race: Samuel and Aldrete, the guys to respect here.

In the next half kilometer they're gone for good. Making this move too early is highly effective if you have the pace to go the entire road. But it is also the toughest thing to pull off like this. It is well known you shouldn't go with them; it will be a yo-yo pacing through the toughest part of the race until you're dead. From these two, I'm only competing against Samuel. I think there are still three places left if I stay here.

On the other hand, I'll end up the anonymous twenty place overall. All I can do is accept it. I can only do what I came here to do and stick to my plan.

Kilometer 12

Halfway through the long straight I've ended up at the front of our group, reduced now to nine runners. I'm in second place to qualify for the university games behind Samuel. That's where I'm staying. If I can run a constant pace all the way through it will also be a PB for me.

From the nine runners sitting behind me, the four leading women have better PB's than mine. The other three are a veteran, Gustavo and Aaron and another guy I haven't seen before. They are running side by side.

Aaron is running smoothly but with a hellish pace. Gustavo seems to be a bit under pressure to keep the pace. The sweat in his face starts to reveal the pain he is going through to keep it up.

Stuck behind me are the blond girl and one of the Mexican female athletes whose face I recognize from the athletic magazines. It seems as if they are following my pace. Gradually I find a better cadence between my strides and relax my arms and elbows. Running a long straight is a gradual increase of tempo, like being in trance; you have to feel you're pushing the tarmac away with every stride.

Another horse is on the side of the road and two skinny cows further afield. It feels very rural with no buildings close by. Luckily enough there is no wind; otherwise this straight section would be just hell.

Kilometer 13

The road is narrow and there are almost no spectators. Everything here has to do with the flatness of the tarmac. The sun warms it up. A yellow mark on the right indicates we've just gone through 13km and a bit. The entire course is marked by this yellow stripe that bends through the roads as if looking for the shortest route. The great Ken Pike used to say that if you were to follow the line on a marathon course you might end up running ten more meters at the end. What are ten meters after forty two thousand and one hundred and ninety five meters! Typical math eccentricities of this great coach.

I'm running strong and relaxed. Too strong for this early part of the race. I'll have to slow down a bit. But if

I slow down gently when the long straight is over I should have made some damage to the group and my position will be secure. Interview with Will Cockerell, runner from England, after a very fast race: "His pace was devastating all the way" Meaning: he ran smoothly and relaxed all the way, no surges.

I slow down a bit. Felt great. How on earth can I abstract my mind and talk to myself during a race?

Kilometer 14

At last the long straight section seems to be ending. Some glimpses of trees on the horizon. Still pushing the pace together with one of the female athletes; her style is very similar to the Japanese runners: very short strides and arms moving quite fast. I try to look at her face; she seems to be in a kind of trance as if she can feel the power of her legs smoothly launching forward as efficiently as possible.

The other two female athletes seem to not care that one is pushing the pace. It would appear that between them there is no challenge at all but this is far from true. They are like scorpions waiting for the others to show some weakness, and then the strongest will bite lethally with a surge that the others won't be able to match.

For the first time in the race I can feel the sweat on my face. This is good, until now I haven't lost too much water. From now on I need to start drinking a bit more water and I make a mental note of this. During the Windsor Half Marathon of 2000, I missed two drinking stations that cost me five places. Never skip the drinking station when it is hot and you will be running for more than an hour: this is one of many things you learn the hard way.

Kilometer 15

Another split is given, courtesy of the digital clock standing on top of a truck. Just under 52 minutes. Spot on.

I can feel a sudden loss of stamina; is it an illusion? Or is this some kind of depletion of my energy levels? It is too early to hit the wall, I think. The signs are clear: quick sweat, feeling a bit dizzy and difficulty to keep the pace. I concentrate on my arms and elbows –this has worked before. And try to exaggerate the swing so as to relax my breathing. My head is betraying me and I try to look around to see if anybody in the group has realized this temporal disadvantage I have. But nobody cares.

Everyone is worried about their own things and strategies. The race is still in an early stage and there will be plenty of time to check on other runners later.

Two minutes since it started. I have managed to keep the pace but at the back of the pack. I hope nobody noticed this, although the blond girl did look at me when I slowed down. I need to gain time. It will be gone in two more minutes or so, and then I can pick up the pace again. We are now almost at the end of the long straight. There is a nice green field which is visually striking, as everything else is quite dry and brownish.

A drinking station is coming up; shall I slow the pace even more and try to get a good sip of water? 'Lazo be aggressive', I keep repeating to myself. The great Paul Evans once lost a race for slowing down at the drinking station. Later he would recognize the dilemma you normally have when you urgently need water in your system and yet this will create a gap between the people you are racing and yourself. It takes a good surge to get back to them in the next few meters so they cannot take advantage and pull away. The real guesswork is to find out if the other runners are taking liquids at the same time.

I get closer to one side and grasp a small cup almost without spilling. This is a balancing act: keep moving your legs and arms and bring the cup closer to your mouth to swallow water. Nice short symphony and I sip two good shots.

Kilometer 16

The strength is slowly coming back. I can feel this in my legs as the stride gets longer and longer but with less effort. Good, I can get back at the front of the group. I don't like running at the back. In many ways it is dangerous. It is like being in a cycling race in the middle of the peloton.

As we make a left turn into a dual carriageway my body is fully recovered and my mind shifts focus to the next five kilometers. We need to start making some damage to this group; everybody seems comfortable and not willing to pick up the pace and see what happens. The last kilometer marker indicates: Torreon 7. I remember that one. It means the return to the city, and it should be close to the point where we will make a turn and start coming back through a different road.

Four more kilometers to the half way point. I put my hand in my small pocket and pull out my half gummy bear. One of the women is sweating and all I can see is the sweat on her half naked back. I'm barely sweating. Lazo: feel no pain at all.

Two more bends and we can see a runner from the back. He will come towards us; possibly in a couple of minutes he will be swallowed up by our group. One of the great feelings a runner has is to see runners falling back. This feeling changes as the race evolves. Funny – you become more of a comrade as the marathon progresses.

Kilometer 17

There is a curve, and after that I see more open fields with dogs around; the end of nothing and a glimpse of more boring straight road ahead. Aaron surges to the end of the bend. He is at the front of the pack now probably because his style is like a yo-yo and because he wants to follow my example and be at the front all the time. He's forgotten that there is still almost half of the distance to come. The rest of the kilometer seems to go in a few seconds. Gosh, I wish this could be the same for the rest of the race.

Kilometer 18

A brisk wind comes in at an angle and hits us in the face. Not bad, it's refreshing and dries up our sweat. There are some clouds to the right and the trees indicating a long avenue still to come.

Suddenly I see a slow runner coming up towards me; there is a cyclist beside him, as if talking to him. I can't recognize his vest. He must be one who went with the leading pack and paid the price.

The wind has slowed down. I look around to see how compact the group is; almost instinctively I try to put someone behind. I make some signs and wave my hand: "come on, let's work together to catch more runners" I say.

That is the brave attitude every runner should have. At least it's the Mexican soul of a fighter for anything. I look ahead to find a spot where I will slow down and wait for someone else to go to the front and pull the group. As I'm thinking this, the Blond girl passes me. Now we are working.

The runner we caught is long gone. We can spot another running casualty in the distance. Whenever I'm at the front of the group I try to see which vest he has. A little over ninety seconds gap to catch him. He is also with a cyclist at his side. Is he trying to get some advice? Impossible, it's too late, he is coming backwards.

How long has he been running on his own? One by one the group keeps pushing the pace: the two girls, then the Blond, then the three veterans and Lazo. All except Aaron who seems not to bother to work as ga roup; we are like cyclists, rotating to keep up the speed. I have to keep an eye on him.

The eight of us are fighting to get these dropped runners. Pulling to the front is the hardest part but when somebody else comes through, the slow down feels fantastic. We work together without a word, but not Aaron. He is just hanging at the back, having a ride.

Kilometer 19

The fields are slightly green here. Fenced on one side, the fields seem like Dutch landscapes, organized and well managed. The road gets narrower but almost flat and straight. It is not as long as the previous one but feels very long. The sky ahead is dark blue. No spectators and almost an hour and a quarter to go.

We pass another dropped runner. Also running on his own, like a hero returning from battle; he doesn't make the effort to stay with us, as if his race is only for the first half. Could he be a rabbit? We can hear some music in the distance. Could it be from the leading car? Impossible.

One of the veterans blows his nose. Half lands on the tarmac while the other goes straight to the calf of one of the Kenyan women. I don't understand these veterans. They keep running this hard knowing they will finish with a time much slower than their PB's. Some of them will also suffer at the very end of this race but still they do it and they are as wise as wolfs when it comes to race tactics. But they are not racing against me.

Kilometer 20

Almost sixty two minutes. Still I'm not racing badly, that amazes me every time. It hurts, but it's also sort of nice. I have a thought: heavy task to deliver a good kiss on a rough night to your girlfriend in her car.

Keep pushing here. The way I see it, your running shoes are light and smooth and you just have to let them go with each stride. You need strong legs for that. The sweat goes down my calf down to my ankle and then disappears. Water runs down my legs, sweeping my hair on its way, my legs looks incredibly muscular.

I run hard. My breathing is calm and normal; no gasp or roughness on my throat. When running, sometimes it's hard to know when your lungs are going to say: Stop, that's all I can do for you today. The mind is clever enough to ask your body to reduce the speed and effort so that you don't collapse. That is the great challenge: to trick your own mind and discover the limits of your body.

What can I do but admire myself? This is instinctive to any animal. I hear nothing and see nothing, but I sense that behind me, every runner is falling behind. Not long ago, while training with Dionisio Ceron, I asked how he could react to people coming behind him. "I always come from behind and make sure nobody is with me", he said.

I hesitate but slowly turn my head to look behind all the other runners being dropped. I glance and realize everybody is amazed at how hard the pace is. Sharp and strong that Lazo, look at him.

Am I dreaming or can I see the gap closing on Samuel and Aldrete?

My athletic history
July 1997

Father's day is not always very important in Mexico. It doesn't have the same profound meaning of Mother's day –it's rather more a fake celebration, dull and meaningless but nevertheless it is a celebration and it is always the third Sunday in July. On that day, a famous athletic club of the city celebrates this with a half marathon race taking over one of the most important roads in the city, the so-called Periferico. It is a day when it's closed for cars, and pedestrians take over this amazing eight lane highway.

It's generally attended by good runners from central México, and throughout the years it has produced thrilling races and exciting comebacks as well as gruelling nasty experiences. I was ready to break my PB, not because it was an easy course or because I was in excellent shape, but for the purely insane feeling of being stronger on father's day. It was going to be the first race that my family would be watching and you always feel this, even those assholes who claim they don't.

It was a rainy early morning; the start was disorganized as usual, extending the warming up time and making everything before the start really uncomfortable; my mind was focused on one thing only: ready to roll, though the first few miles were going to be fast. And they were extremely fast.

After 34min running, the 10k mark was gone, the long wide highway was a river of people and at the front the police motorcycles were playing zigzag on the open road like kids in a new playground. The leading group was compact; I was about 100 metres behind running solid and hard, feeling good and passing runners who had started too quick in the downhill of the first 5k. By the turn, when you know that you have to go back, uphill all the way, you better keep something in the fuel tank. I still felt my legs were strong and good, I would probably have a real chance of breaking my PB.

The hardest part of the hill comes as you come next to a huge shopping centre crowded with people buying presents. It feels good to have people cheering you up – although they are there for other reasons.

Half way 21.1km

The second long straight is over. Two more kilometers and the flyovers will start. It's warm. My brain is ready to burn like hot potatoes. Running hard that entire straight road at the front of the group I felt like the front of the train going towards the abyss.

We're also closing in on Samuel and Aldrete. The gap is around 90 meters, but I can tell now that we will get them before the 25k mark for sure. I take another strong stride and my brain temperature rises again. Still my breathing is very relaxed and I'm not gasping. This is good and I get ready to spit once again.

The drinking station comes up. There are lots of people pushing each other to shout at us. The leading elite women have their own table with special drinks; from the rest of the group, hands come towards the tables and grab whatever they can. Some of the volunteers even try to run for a few meters to help us: it's useless, they don't run fast enough.

Gustavo's running style has become clunky. It could be a blister or a damaged calf, I think. He's almost at the point of limping but still manages to keep the pace and get to the back of the group.

Suddenly he drops back five meters. We're about to cross the carpet of the half-way point and he's almost six meters behind.

How many of us are there now? At the 10k mark we were almost twenty runners. Now we're seven, eight? I'm afraid to look back and loose my pace.

During my training sessions with Aaron and Gustavo, they both had already dropped me long before this. Aaron is the fastest here today, he's tall and skinny. On weekdays he's studying to become a film maker. You wouldn't think he is this good a runner when he's wearing his normal clothes. He just looks like a leftist student hanging around the art school for too long. He started running when he was seventeen but he wasn't fast enough for the middle distance, although in every training session he thinks he can still run a fast track race.

There's always a secret ingredient to the way he races. A strong carrot cake made by his mum the day before, a super fast pace in his legs, his lungs feeling incredibly strong. I don't really know, but he always has that extra to pull off. He doesn't mind it when I curse him. He takes a lot from me because we're friends.

"Hey Aaron what kind of trick or good excuse you're going to pull out now, rat?" "Did you have some power booster tequilas yesterday?" He looks at me and says that I should wait and see.

I'm absolutely right, he's cooking something.

"Wait for the 30km; don't push too hard before then".

I don't believe him for a minute, I should be ready at any time.

Nevertheless he is not as strong and hard minded a runner. On long races he runs well against the odds but he has never won a race because there is always someone faster or stronger than him. He has the stamina to keep going.

He lives to run or, does he run to live?

All of a sudden, two runners come and stay beside me. I turn quickly and look at them. They aren't from my qualifying group but still it means TWO more places if they finish ahead. Who are they? How did they gain on us? They must have pushed very hard during the last five kilometers. I see one of them has a foreign vest but looks young. Maybe inexperience, I think. Their breathing doesn't sound very comfortable, the other guy's shoulders are all over the place; he's tired but still pushing. He has squandered his strength by going with this youngster. He can't stick to him, of course, and he won't be able to stick with us. He is going to die soon.

As I accelerate a bit, I move half a meter ahead of these two and Aaron is coming with me too. I will have a good race with him. The two Kenyan women are also behind and close together, with the blond girl another meter adrift. Today won't be the day I bite the dust of these two.

It's because we're running alongside the leading women group that people are clapping and cheering. How many times have I been in this situation before, where the enthusiasm is more for the leading women who are running comfortably among male pace makers? Anyway this is the way it is. The men's winner will never get the right level of applause unless the first woman comes beside him.

The first flyover is coming up, with a long steep incline. I'm not going to slow down, though, I relax my arms and raise my heels, and I'm pushing it. It's so incredibly pitiful that I ever wanted to do this, but now I'm stuck with it.

Kilometer 22

Another motorcycle passes by in search of the leaders, I presume. It disappears under the flyover and beyond. There is always the feeling of how slow you really run when you see a vehicle that close going fast enough to lose it in seconds. And what is their speed? 30 kilometers an hour, maybe? We pass two runners who have dropped out. Rabbits maybe; they only race for money. One is a Kenyan. There weren't many Kenyans in Mexico before but now they seem to be in every race. And they win.

Every time I have done a marathon I get the same routine when I reach the point of having run more than what is left. A vision of the glass half full, I believe. First comes the anxiety of a self assessment, critical enough to not fool yourself about how much is left in the tank. Paul Evans used to declare that his strategy was always of negation: the first half of every marathon should be erased from your memory when you start the second half. A great lie.

In the mind of every runner there is, at this moment, the confusion about how to run the next 9 kilometers knowing that when you reach the 30km mark the real marathon starts. The head spins making calculations that in the end are a mere illusion. What is left is almost the same distance as what you have done, except that you are tired already. To remind you of this, generally there is a big mark on the pavement.

Kilometer 23

Major developments: in front of me, Samuel is dropping back. Aldrete is about a hundred meters ahead of him. He is continuing on his own. Hang on. I'm between one of the female Kenyans and Aaron. My legs are sweating a lot. Samuel is not looking good now, he is visibly slowing down, and we catch up with him and then leave him behind. He doesn't even bother to chase us or stick to the back of the group. I can tell it wasn't his day. That is the way it is with him. He has run this marathon five times. A year he finishes in the top three and the next he drops out. And so it will be. He will be lucky if he can finish this one. Now I remember, Samuel ran another marathon three weeks ago and came fifth. He shouldn't have been here today. That's why they call him the *donkey*.

Aldrete is gone. I can barely see him now; the Kenyan woman is pushing the pace harder -she wants to get rid of some competition in the women's race; I don't see the other Kenyan nor the Mexicans, the blond girl is just behind, running smoothly, arms relaxed and almost no sweat on her belly.

We're moving like a single body, well packed together. At every flyover the incline gets the grip and we loose contact but then on the down slope we are well packed again.

I need to get some pace. Four flyovers gone, four to go. We just passed the 23km mark. Someone shouts, "Top fifteen, keep going… doing well". How many of us are still in this group? Don't look around. How fast are we going anyway? I should check on the last kilometer, I glimpse at my watch and see: three twenty two.

For the first time we are running one behind the other: the two Kenyan women, Aaron, Gustavo, and behind me, the blond girl.

Kilometer 24

Entering back into Torreon, there is some tail wind and still two more flyovers to come. The blond girl just came on my side, she's wearing sunglasses; "good thinking" I say. She turns slightly, nods her head and pushes on. Jesus, another flyover uphill is coming up. There is a sense of emptiness on this part of the course. Not very nice to be standing on a flyover I think, even if there are no cars. The motorcycle with the camera crew is closely following the women's race.

When at the end of her career, they asked the great Norwegian runner Greta Waitz about her greatest marathon. She didn't mention any of the nine wins in New York City, nor her win at the 1983 world championship race in Helsinki. She spoke about the Olympic marathon in 1984.

She couldn't win that one, but that's why she chose it. What Waitz had always loved about that race was that she was beaten by her closest friend and training partner Joan Benoit Samuelson. Both, when training, had thought about the potential fight they would have one day; during the 75 miles a week or more of training, they always tried to find each other's weakest point. Waitz ran fast the first half of the Olympic race in 84 in the hope that she would break Samuelson. She didn't count on the hot and humid weather conditions that morning in LA.

Wonderful images: Waitz, pushing hard on every stride, with every one of the contestants fading back in the Santa Monica area, except the small figure of Samuelson. Photos of Samuelson passing Waitz, in pain; and Waitz trying to stay with Samuelson.

When Waitz was coming into the Coliseum, she could hear the roar of the Americans cheering Samuelson. Instead she was so drained that she even slowed down and jogged the last kilometer. Waitz was dehydrated and exhausted, but had won her first Olympic silver medal.

Kilometer 25

Last flyover, one Kenyan woman dumped, Gustavo dumped, Samuel dumped, and you name it! The second Kenyan woman, dumped. Two women contending to win the marathon and three men left competing for the places in the national team: Aaron, Aldrete and me. Five runners in total. I try not to think of this and focus my mind on the fields we pass by; they are dry and yellow and some light green. Keep my mind on something else I keep repeating, but suddenly my focus comes back to this moment.

'Let's go for Aldrete' I shout. He is about a hundred meters in front. We have a huge gap to the next group behind. We are all running close by. A sharp turn right is followed but another left turn which is taking us to the nice part of the city: the golf club district. It's difficult to find an easy rhythm; we're all pulling at slightly different paces, here and there, drifting from one side of the road to the other, looking for the shade of trees, the sun is very strong on the road. And Aldrete seems to have stopped! He is stretching and bending down. All of a sudden, that gap is closing in seconds. We pass him, but I see him starting to run just as we pass him. I try to pick up the pace hoping he finds it difficult to stay with us.

Aaron has been in the middle of our small group all the time. I glance over to see if he is willing to do the hard work for a while, and of course, he doesn't. Bastard!

This guy sometimes annoys me. In a marathon you have to run in a group at some point. That's the whole idea, to be clever and save energy from time to time. The Mexican woman is working, I'm working, and the blond girl is working, so why is Aaron not doing it?

Kilometer 26

But trying to slow down and let him take the lead would just slow us all down. It would cost us valuable seconds. 'Goddamn it, Aaron, if you just want to sit there and wait why don't you say it straight away', I say. He looks at me and pulls back to the very back with Aldrete, the never changing smile on his face. No matter how difficult the race conditions are, the same naughty boy smile.

We're approaching the twisting part of the course around the golf course. Should I give him some more hell? It's too early in the race to pick a fight. But the anger in me seems to give me more fuel. And in fact, if he holds on to my surge I will have to do all the work. At least in the group there are more legs.

A sign indicates we're entering the Golf club area. A thermometer marks 28 degrees Celsius. Every time I'm at the front of the group, I feel it: I'm strong today. So what if I surge here? Then my chances later would be reduced.

Correct.

After an hour and a half of running, my legs are in the top fifteen of the marathon of LALA. I like to be in this position at the beginning of a ten kilometer race, but today is different.

Kilometer 27

A sharp right turn is in sight with a big nice red brick house on the left. It looks like I could make some good proposals to the owner to refurbish it but I think we would have a few discrepancies about style. One side of the house seems to be imported from the Alps, with its sloped roof and huge windows.

The narrower road along the Golf club is twisting along a line of houses where a few people are coming out to see the race. There is some shade for the first time and I find myself on the edge of the kerb as if to get the most of it. I've made sure I'm at the front of the group. It is going to be harder to get ahead on this narrow road. I increase my speed.

The runner in the foreign vest all of a sudden is back but he's tired. I can see that in his face. Why do some people suffer to live running while others run to live suffering? This guy is limping, is it a blister? Difficult to say, but I stay focused and try not to look too much at him. Just before the next kilometer mark he's gone, and God help him from here until the finish line. It is going to be hell for him.

Another two runners have dropped out. Good place to do it, I think. The drinking station is not far away and the shade of the trees will keep them fresh, if they can move I mean. Why not ask some of the residents for some breakfast and a shower? That would be lovely. My despair has no limits today. Poor guys, they are drained and I should have compassion for them.

Kilometer 28

Sign: *Torreon Jardin* exit 500 meters. A row of houses –or small chalets I should say are courting us through the golf course. This should mean that we are entering the dead zone of the race; a place where nothing seems to move apart from your legs.

Kilometers pass by but the omniscient 30 km mark still to come and the half way is long gone. I hate comparisons but this is where a cycling road race and a marathon differ. The former has the intermediate prizes or premiums, in the latter there is no reward until you have really finished. I remember someone saying that the cyclist Miguel Indurain used to think that the Tour de France is like a marathon that lasts sixteen days. No individual stage prizes for him, then.

I'm onto one of the girls' tail. Aaron is still behind but soon he'll make his move. He is not gaining anything now by staying behind. His legs have come the same distance except he has not made any mental effort.

What I expect is exactly what's happening now: Aaron is going to suffer as well. I need to look carefully at his face. His expression will change soon and then I should react and push – Lazo is like a killer bee.

Kilometer 29

Out of the corner of my eye, a blue-yellow glimpse: it's the blond girl trying to get past me; I force myself to make another surge and she drops back. There is a sign. It says that there are some bumps ahead, another headache I think, first the reduced space on the road, then all the turns and now this; my head is just exploding and my lungs start to feel dry.

Turn to the left, turn to the right, watched by big families in swimming suits. And the straight sector of the Golf club house ahead. Someone shouts:

"You are the second group, well done, ten kilometers to go!"

I try to catch a glimpse of my coach. The cheering has a *norteño* sound; we're not the first ones to come through here and one of the favorites is a local runner.

Here we go again. The turns continue, but now the sun is facing us. We regroup but I feel someone in the group is going to get dropped. Five kilometers still to go in the Golf club area and then we will be out towards the centre of Torreon. Pain, I still have to go through the wall. After these next few kilometers I hope to feel better.

Aaron is beside Gustavo. I follow them; the blond girl follows me a little to one side. The next few turns are gentle and with a small down incline. I feel that on my legs. Now that Aldrete is gone I notice the gap with

47

the leaders thanks to a clock installed beside the road. One of the leaders has just dropped back and I can see him going through the showers installed in the course. It's hot, but he appears to almost stop inside.

We pass the showers. No one goes in; I'm sure we all think the same: water in the shoes and the blisters can come in 2 kilometers. The mark of the 30 Km is almost there. I feel my racers are still in perfect condition and my arches are still well supported. My flat feet seem to be always present, as a promise of pain to come. After all, why not choose a less painful sport? The marathon is the worst thing for flat feet. It's been a while since I've run in this type of hot weather –thankfully it's not humid, otherwise I would be silently running while my whole body sweats.

Kilometer 30

The mythical mark appears almost by surprise. A policeman is stopping the traffic as we pass by. He points to the right to the driver as we see a row of palm trees and some shade. Another dropped runner who seems to have an elite number and his face is covered in sweat. I can almost see the drops of sweat hit the pavement and immediately evaporate. This is something interesting about marathon distance: no matter how good you are, even if you are the favorite, you can still feel an inexplicable pain and stop, slow down or drop out.

A gentle down slope feels like glory. Not too steep so that it could hurt but enough to relax the arms and stretch a bit.

The two Kenyan women start to disappear at this point. A strange feeling and some butterflies make this departure a bit sad. When you have been running together for almost an hour and fifty minutes you have made some kind of companionship. Dave Bedford couldn't win the London marathon on his own: he crossed the line with his mate as a sign of absurd friendship in perhaps the only marathon that has witnessed a double winner result. I bet he wouldn't have done that if it had been the Olympic marathon. The two girls appear to be tired all of a sudden. We didn't make any surge or increase the pace; it was a simple but painful slowdown in her legs.

In conversation with other runners, the same thing always comes up: the best part was the suffering. In Toluca I once trained with the Ecuadorian runner Silvio Guerra who was living in Mexico. A real fighter but never a winner. He used to do sessions that could kill a cheetah and he was the best at high altitude training but when it came to the marathon he didn't have the character to break the opposition. Another example of great attitude but defeat by pain: Vincent Roseau, marathon record man, never accepted to run a marathon if the temperature was higher than 22 degrees.

Kilometer 31

The wall comes almost when I thought it would. Just as we are leaving the golf club area, a flat long straight appears and with that my legs are just gone. It is the moment every runner hates and expects to come; an ever present karma of what we are and how fragile we could become in seconds.

I have been racing in hot weather before with Aaron near the coast of Veracruz. He came up to me and said do you fancy a shower race? With a smile on his face, the tall and skinny figure was definitely being sarcastic. In the end I discover how each body copes differently with hot weather. Except for the fact that I later discovered what was his specialty: short races. He was the perfect five mile runner: skinny, tall, resisting hot track conditions, but when he tried the marathon a few years later he succumbed. This was when we became really good friends. All that was left of his resistance to hot weather was his irony before any race.

No matter where you do a marathon, after 30 kilometers the expressions on the faces of every runner are all the same. They all appear to be thinking of something very deep and important. But it is just that: a cover for a deeper and more serious transformation and depletion of your body energy.

Almost at the end of the long straight a car appears on one of the side streets. There is a slight curve but I manage to see it's one of those old GM Impalas. I'm allowed to see it. Even if it is to forget the drain on my legs that I hope will last almost four minutes before I start to recover. For the first time in the race I take a look at the blond girl's running number: 329 it reads in bold black figures with a green and white background. I doubt lucky numbers exist in the marathon. The entire mystique that we can attribute to those digits is purely a mental trick to hope for the best result possible sometimes beyond our real capability. The only number that perhaps could mean something is: ONE.

Kilometer 32

After the curve is another straight with nice palm trees in the middle. The blond girl is still here –as if we both have hit the wall at the same time. The marathon is the cruelest of the races. A marathon runner's body can only cope for a few years – the great Spanish runner Martin Fiz used to say no more than eight. You do have the occasional prodigy, who appears to last more. In 1978 the 18 year old Alberto Salazar was one of those. He went on to be one of the first to run six marathons in one year during 1981. But a year later he succumbed during the New York Marathon. He won, but he never recovered.

At the end of the palm tree-lined road I see the finish line –silly me, there is still a 10k loop to the park. Just as we turn, a runner from the leading pack is coming towards us.

This is just before a small incline in sight, right when I think, very soon I will have to make a surge. Almost halfway though this last kilometer, the wall is gone, I feel strong, and my legs are back. Just at this point, Gustavo slows down and, as if by intuition, I slow the pace as well. The blond girl takes the lead of the small group, Aaron is behind us, and I'm second in the group.

A few meters ahead a sign indicates: "centro derecho". The buildings alongside the road have more shops and restaurants - do I feel hungry? We are back in the centre of the city, I think. That means that no more hills or flyovers will come; now I must concentrate on the rhythm of the pace but at the same time, this is the hardest part of the race. This is the point when good runners start to look over their shoulders to see the expression in the faces of their contenders. Just to find the right time to attack. Sometimes you reach the end of something only because you forget for a moment that it isn't over yet.

Just as we make a turn, we're keeping an eye on each other. Could it be true that none of us is now interested in beating each other? It is just a matter of running against the clock, beating your personal mark, but one must also ensure your pride is not hit by somebody else breaking you apart in the last part of the race.

My athletic history
April 1996

On a warm early morning I received an invitation to attend the Paralympic Games. All I needed to do was to be a guide for a blind runner in the 10,000 meters race – a real medal contender. How fanciful is that? His name was Alejandro Guerrero and I had met him a couple of years before while training in the mountains near Toluca in Mexico. We came across each other in a few races and it happened that I always managed to beat him by about a minute difference but he was always ahead of me at the start. He was disappointed with his guide at the time. His complaint was that he could run faster with a faster guide. I became part of his equation.

Almost nine months before the Olympics, the championship to select who would go as part of the Mexican team was held. The venue was Veracruz –the same horrible hot and humid place where a few years before, I was racing against Aaron in the national 5000 meters championship, a defeat that I will never forget.

But that warm morning –of the Paralympics selection, nothing was going to stop us, Alejandro and his guide –Lazo, from beating everybody and setting a new Mexican record for a disabled athlete. There we go. I lived somebody else's dream of winning an Olympic medal.

Kilometer 33

Four hundred meters to climb I reckon. It is not a steep hill but nevertheless it's a long slope that will kill our legs. Where the hell did that come from? Holding together, we carry our tired legs up the slope. I glance back and catch a glimpse of Aaron 5 meters behind us. When I look again, he's closer, I thought we might have dumped him but no, he is coming back. He has character. The top of the incline is crowned by a group of nice girls in minis. I see a short, petit brunette in the middle of the group. "Vamos, ya les falta poco", she shouts "tu les ganas".

Why is she shouting that?

She knows how a marathon race is. And she probably saw the leaders already. She knows then that the blond girl is the leading woman but our race is not against her. She has no idea of what 33 kilometers in the legs are.

What gives this girl the right to raise her voice?

It is four runners she has just seen but her shouts are for the blond girl. A feminist perspective possibly, from a girl in her youth, who backs the woman racing against the sports establishment. As soon as I pass by her, I realize she is beautiful, but I hate her.

Still a few meters to the top of the slope, and painted on the road in blue letters is a sign that says: ULTIMOS 10 K. That means we are entering the cruelest part of a marathon, the unknown zone. This is the centre of Torreon, not many slopes in the city, so a good road circuit for runners.

I've run through the calculations a few times, and now I know with a good degree of certainty: there can only be eleven runners ahead in the leading pack. No idea how far ahead they are but I hope only one or two from my category. In our group there are four including, I suspect, the leading women; Aaron, who is my only real direct competitor and Gustavo.

Of the original group running for the two hours thirty mark, it's only us now. The last third of the race is going to be serious running. This is where a good time is achieved. My legs are soaking wet, as are my short and my vest. Almost all the water I drink goes out straight away. As a consolation, I can see the other runners in the group are in the same situation: the blond is holding a sponge and Gustavo still has a bottle in his hand from the last drinking station.

Kilometer 34

Aaron and the blond girl make a small surge in front. Aaron is moving his arms straight and up, almost exaggerating, but he looks strong and light, almost floating a few centimeters off the ground. Apart from the bad patch at the 31 kilometer, he has been running well so far. The blond girl, in contrast, seems to be suffering. Her arms don't look relaxed, her head is all over the place.

A flat section, the sticky blackness of the pavement is in front, a crowd on both sides and some shops or restaurants as urban background. A couple of VW Beetles are parked on one side with a big yellow balloon floating above them. LUCOZADE it reads. The sponsors always seem to find the strangest places to put their adverts. Gustavo passes the kilometer mark first, as if this was a bonus line in Le Tour, he is not a good climber but he's fast on the downhill. He has forgotten this is a flat bit.

There is no shade and it's feeling hot; exactly what I didn't want. The next water station is still one kilometer away; I can't see yet which side of the road it will be on.

And suddenly I see, in front of us, twenty meters away, another runner dropped. It is the guy form Club Viveros, another direct competitor for me. A bit of tailwind and I pick up the pace: "come on guys" I think, "let's do it swiftly and quickly so he can't stay with us".

This has come as a real bonus for me. In a way, once this guy is behind, unless a catastrophe occurs, Aaron and I are qualified. I can't take any risks. I need to keep pushing.

Why is the marathon this exact distance? Why? Blame Queen Victoria.

Kilometer 35

A sign indicates we're almost in the city centre. I'm just behind Gustavo, holding and holding the pace. My legs feel okay but my breathing is not regular and calm, I feel strange butterflies in my right arm. The blond girl is stretching our small group. What I expected is exactly what's happening now: Aaron is going to get burst, he is hitting the wall. A couple of meters behind, Gustavo speeds up and I'm behind him, saving energy and protecting myself from the wind. The end of our group is here. In a flash, I look back, only to see Aaron being left in pieces, struggling and swinging his neck like a parrot. It is a strange feeling but I feel happy to have hit the wall early on.

The Blond girl hammers away; this is looking like a full sprint. It seems she has recovered: her arms are more relaxed and her stride is strong. She is pulling away but it's nothing more than a push of the soul. Things here don't get around by thinking without reacting. I feel pain in my left foot. I'm not entirely sure, but it could be a blister; maybe another nail will go.

People are lining both sides of the road; the finish line is less than ten kilometers away. Now I'll show Gustavo what a push is about, and I start passing him, but my legs get such a fright that I grant him the lead again. He has also worked hard so far, so he deserves to lead the way still. The motorcycle with the cameraman is getting closer to us. I suppose this is how it's going to be the last few kilometers. The blond girl is getting all the attention and we are two pace makers for her.

No matter how many runners you ask, they will always answer that the last seven kilometers of a marathon are the most difficult and important. This is where the good times are achieved or hopes are destroyed.

Kilometer 36

A bit of the downhill stretch to the centre of the Torreon which I have been looking for the last twenty minutes and been running for two hours, just twenty five minutes or so to go. Lazo and Gustavo lead the second group with the blond girl.

"Easy now", the blond says. Uff, that's a relief; we both ease off a little and relax the arms. A drinking station is coming up, I will need to take a sip and maybe grab a sponge as well. Straight ahead is the main street where the leading group must be. I turn back again and see Aaron almost a hundred meters behind; he seems to be trying to come back. Is this the next decisive moment? On paper, Gustavo is a better middle distance runner than I am. He surely will have the advantage if we keep on like this. Should I push again and try to break him, to lose him once and for all, and risk having to do another sprint if he recovers in the final meters?

I slow down, Gustavo takes over, and the Blond Girl comes beside me. The pace is steady and the water station is gone but I managed to get the much needed water and isotonic drink. I give some to Gustavo and he passes this to the blond. Nice team work, I think for a second. We are now a very small group of three running on the shady side of the road with people shouting "vamos falta poco...". A cloud gives some extra shade. We're on a wide road, buildings on the side and some cowboy restaurants advertising some kind of Vegas style casino. A dog. It is not watching.

Kilometer 37

I run. I'm once again able to communicate my feelings to the state of mind I am in: I got it. I will finish top of the group to qualify for the world university games, that's amazing but I will not break my personal best and may not beat Gustavo. I give everything, but of course Gustavo is doing the same and that makes him stand a better chance in the final meters. I can't do any more; I really can't do any more. This is the moment when the mind can defeat you if you are not sensible.

Honking and shouting there is Evert, my coach, "te ves como una vaca" he's shouting. He probably wants me to speed up. Precisely what I can't do. He is fond of me, I have been with him for five years and I have grown to become something of a runner. I have won races for his club; I'm his very own 'niño mágico'.

But hey, Evert, I'm only giving it everything I've got because no one says I have to. Only when there are arguments for something can there be are arguments against it. The only time I have abandoned a race for lack of morale was when someone had gone with me especially to watch.

The legs are hurting. No matter how easy I breathe, I can't relax and get more air into my lungs. Gustavo will come from behind. No, I can't do it any more now. That's right; I'm not even supposed to be able to do it any more. Let them go, even the Blond girls, they are beyond your remit.

All my training and mileage over the last few months, that was a joke, of course. Maybe it did go a little too far: too many weekly miles. It was wonderful, though, that having started at the age of twenty six I was still able to get a body that could really do something, that managed to run under thirty one minutes for a ten kilometer race amid a hundred hungry youngsters, that won occasionally in lesser races. It was fantastic enough to have taught any number of these glory boys a lesson in strength, in courage, in character.

The shade is gone, and a girl in a blue and yellow vest passes me. It's the blond girl sprinting. I don't know how to react.

Kilometer 38

Gustavo: twenty eight years old, that guy. I know him, he is still with me. He makes gestures, his arms are firm and his head is upright, his stride is long, calm. He is sweating a lot but still he looks strong. He nods: come on. I wish sometimes people would leave me alone. I run as fast as I can and at least I'm still with him, just behind.

I'm sitting on his back. My legs have started to feel like the 10th round of a boxing fight. Now I'm running faster than I can. Everything tells me I won't be able to stick with him, but since June 17th 1993, pain is no longer a signal to stop. Lazo will go until the end, even if this means his death.

The last few kilometers before the central avenue of Torreon and the central park. No escape here. Gustavo and the blond girl stranded in this fight. How am I going to get rid of this guy and not get defeated by this blond girl? If only I would get another surge. Many times in the past, fighting all the way in a long beaten group that nonetheless sets a fast pace I could barely follow, have I hoped for a surge? Whatever it is, I need permission from my body to regain confidence.

For years, something kept me from talking to other runners about that hope, but when I did turn out they all knew what I was feeling. I regain confidence in my silence as this was shared by other running mates. A lot of thinking goes on in the racing pack, especially about pace and glory. Please get me a surge. But the speed of thinking has its limits, so the runner occasionally resorts to more drastic measures. Leonardo Reyes, an unknown Mexican runner and winner of the Houston Marathon, swings his arms in exaggeration, or makes some long strides; when he has a race to run but no speed or strength, he'll even mount a carefully selected cocktail of ephedrine that is ready to give the much needed boost.

There are runners with gloves and long sleeves who treat bad weather as a surge. Surges can take the weirdest form. Some runners who have raced without gloves consider a gelid snow-filled day as a blessing, or a miracle made present. At the start of the national cross country championship in a park near Bristol, I was extremely tense. There were a multitude of signs that something terrible was about to happen, but not a single excuse not to start. Drizzle, cold and damp weather, very windy, mud up to the knees, hills and uneven surfaces, twists, flat bits, another twist, four laps of the bloody course, all pure hard working running for about forty five minutes. But even though I tagged along quite well in a small group, the tension didn't go away. After nine kilometers and a shout from the great coach, Ken Pike saying "this is only a nice stride for a marathon runner like you!!", I started to push and surge, passing runners like snails, it didn't feel as if doing an effort, just stride after stride my pace was faster and stronger. I gained more than fifty places. A big surge. In my running logbook, under results, I wrote: *inspiration*.

Kilometer 39

With each stride, Gustavo pulls out a new story. One kilometer and we will enter the park to do the final lap and the finish line will be just there. More people are shouting and supporting the runners as we pass a small band playing a "norteña" typical of this place. Nice. The pavement is smooth and nice to run on. In the sky there is no sign of more clouds that could give us some shade for these last three kilometers. The worst of my wall is long gone and I can feel my legs stronger with every stride. I could even try to overtake Gustavo and leave him behind. Just a thought as the reminder of a cramp in my calf during my last race comes to mind.

The music is gone and then all of a sudden this part of the road gets a bit of shade from the trees lining the border of the park. Immediate action is to shift from one side of the road to the other; you can see that the leading pack did just that. Some water bottles appear on this side of the road. And then, a big surprise –Lazo is almost securing the first place of his category and may finish in the top 15th.

The sign for a water station is visible now. The final meters of Avenida Revolucion. In the surroundings the central park of the city appears as a big green space, a group of kids in uniform waves at us and shouts. I get past Gustavo.

Another turn ahead but we are still outside the park. Less shade from the trees and it's feeling a bit too hot; Gustavo comes past me again. He waves his hand encouraging me to pick up the pace. The blond girl is sitting just behind him.

Kilometer 40

City centre: the temperature is 24 degrees Celsius. Two more kilometers, as we pass the last drinking station I have a quick look at what's on offer: oranges, lucozade, and water. That's what I want after running for two hours and fifteen minutes, but I feel good and I don't slow down to take anything. In just ten more minutes the outcome will be known.

By now the leading group has all finished. The speaker at the other end of the park shouts out names and times, but it's difficult to understand. I wonder what the winning time was. Two hours ten minutes perhaps? This is a fast course and the elite runners should be capable of running that sort of time. Even in hot conditions, times here are usually fast. On March 12th, 1997, Dionisio Ceron was running on the same road we are now. Ceron was at the peak of his athletic career, had already won the London Marathon three times in a row –something nobody has repeated since, and was silver medalist at the 95 world athletic marathon and would later go on to finish in the top three places in the Boston and New York marathons. The 1997 Maraton de LALA was going to be his first and last attempt to break the marathon record in Mexico. He was top of the elite runners, with a marginal lag behind Espinoza and Pitayo, both world class marathon runners. At the entrance to Avenidad Revolucion, Ceron geared up the pace and began his final attack. They had been running a negative split and the national record was almost in the bag for the three of them. At the northern corner of the park, Ceron had a ten meter gap over Espinoza, with Pitayo a further five meters back. Both were trying to catch him, and made a big surge. But Ceron bit again and increased the pace. No place to go, this was his last victory. He would never win a marathon again. It was perhaps such an effort that he never recovered after this victory, which meant a national record which still stands.

The motorcycle is now joined by two more with TV cameras. This is going to be a big win for the blond girl. She has beaten the two Kenyans, pre race favorites I suppose.

Kilometer 41

A right turn, I'm going behind the blond girl. Someone shouts to her saying she is the leading woman. Apparently Maria del Carmen Diaz, the 'atomic ant', dropped out.

A white concrete wall encloses the central park of the city allowing sight of the trees behind with their green leaves. They are pines I think. I feel I can speed up and surge, getting side by side with the blond. I'm not having any trouble with my legs and I'm much too tired now to worry about matters of life and death. This is about something completely different: about winning my category and earning a place in the youth national squad. A quick look back shows Gustavo and Aaron a good thirty meters back. But a couple of minutes later, they are just behind. What the hell, I surge again. This was Lazo's amazing attack in the last two kilometers and he's the leader of his category in the Maraton of LALA.

Another right turn, we are at the back of the park; the stands will start to appear very soon. There are people on each side, cheering and shouting with a local band playing some kind of funky melody. I think of a band like U2 playing on one of the roofs across the park. In five minutes the outcome will be known. Always the illusion that somewhere the future is already defined, that you are just not allowed to know it yet. But you are racing into the light.

I look back again. Maybe Gustavo is now resigned to be second in our category. I can't believe that I may have to do a sprint finish after almost 40 kilometers. I keep pushing; the sun is burning my face. The blond girl has also dropped a few meters. A bit of macho mentality and I don't allow a girl to beat me.

Kilometer 42 and one hundred and ninety two meters

The final Kilometer; the last turn is almost visible now, together with some stands on both sides. More trees on this side of the park are casting a nice shade as I pass. I look back and Gustavo is a small dot; he is not coming back and the blond is also visibly slowing down a bit. She is going to win the race anyway in the female category. A great roar is heard as she passes by. Two girls along the road look at me. 'He looks amazingly strong and fit. He is only a few minutes behind the winners' and after 41 kilometers the only thought in my head is that in a few minutes I will find out if I'll be selected to go to the world university games as part of the Mexican team. That's all that matters now. Keep the pace, relax the legs and check there is nobody coming back.

My coach would say keep focused and remember real certainty makes the future. I think of the blond girl again, my running buddy for most of this race, a real winner, so what, shall I sprint her just for pride?

Whenever anyone (men) beat the great Tegla Lourpe from Kenya at the final sprit, she always makes sure they will pay the price on other races and shorter distances, reducing them to a snail pace compared with the speed on her legs.

Almost two hours and twenty seven minutes of running. The crowds are quite big for a small town in the north of Mexico. The last long straight is divided for each category. I won't have the glory of cutting the tape but I can see in the distance they are getting ready for the blond. How nice would that feel?

The finish

As in many races, what remains in your head afterwards are the last few meters. As if your mind was on cyclical exercise of remembering those last few seconds before everything stops and it is over. A big post on one side has "800 meters to go" written on it; my arms feel so relaxed that I can't believe it, and my stride is as long as it could be at this point of the race. The blond is almost a meter behind on my side. She looks tired but she is a winner and she has come back to me. With every breath I take I hear the loudspeaker closer and closer. They have just announced the winner of the Marathon LALA 1996.

The guy in the loudspeaker shouts the number of the runner ahead of me. The only thing that stands between my strides and the finish line is 300 meters. Is it over?

And now I find myself almost at the start of the last part of the straight with a few hundred metres to go; the shouting of hundreds of people along the street rolls and hits me, I almost start to cry and my head is thinking of my own glory. How easy it is to betray reality: you have not won anything; nobody will come and congratulate you. Everything is in your mind but the feeling is amazing. I take a deep breath and start sprinting to the finish line and I can hear the breathing of the blond behind –is she taking this personal?

My sporting career 2005 (in a distant future then)

I organized a running club in my company which was meant to be an amateur thing. The initial small group was made up of a friend of mine who also ran for the same athletic club and two girls who had some potential to become good runners. Just like any corporate challenge, we decided that we had to enter a race in which we could stand a chance to win. A mixed-team category would suit us. Unlike any written destiny, we entered a race in which the chances of winning were reasonably good. All we had to do was to enter and finish the race. It was a short distance race: 5.5 kilometres. Of all the things that prevent the marathon runner from achieving the speed required for this distance, during those 20 minutes or less, pain is not one. Middle distance races are hectic!

Those races have been lost because of a last gasp, lack of relaxed arms and shoulders, not getting in the right pace and keeping it constant. I'm going fast; I will be close to the winner on this one. After almost 19 minutes the race is over. It felt as if nothing had happened although the sweat and tired legs are there. The team won –not because of the male members. Our performance was normal but the girls really put us up there.

Oh dear, the finish line is there. Ten seconds and my legs are feeling the sprint and are in a terrible fight to keep the pace. I try to relax my shoulders and look like an elegant Kenyan runner. A careful observer might think that the Blond and I are neck and neck and that I'm trying not to get beaten by her. The finish line is here and I'm half a stride ahead of her. I know that when I'm willing to go to the end I'll go to the real end. I'll beat her. But a great discouragement takes control of me. What did I ever do to deserve this? This marathon was there for me to beat the first female; sure. It is such a pity.

Kilometre 43

The Blond crosses the line first and I finish just behind her. Roaring and shaking. My eyes start to cry and my tiredness bursts. The Blond is standing waiting for someone to take her chip from her shoe and lifts her arms to stretch. I close my eyes while I give a few steps and open my mouth which is very dry. After my chip is taken I start to walk to the bags holding area. In front of me are the Blond and a few other runners −not more than a dozen. I have to stop because it is a bit crowded with officials and staff organizers. In front of me is the Blond who just turns as I pass by: I have to make a gesture and say "congratulations for your victory" at the same time that I twist my ankle. To the left the massage tent, to the right, a sponsor VIP area where the elite runners −those who have finished - are giving interviews. I walk towards a quiet area and I pass by an old man who seems to be taking some notes sitting on an old Boy Scout chair. I keep walking further towards the changing area hoping to see someone from my team. Someone comes and gives me a goody bag and wraps me with a space blanket. My head is hanging down, my breathing is slow. Two photos are taken of me by surprise.

There is a hand on my shoulder, it's Gustavo. I stop and turn around: "did you get her?"

"No. She beat me by half a stride".

"I could see you crossing the line. I was a minute down from you. I completely drowned with two kilometres to go".

We walk together and then turn around to see another small group finish. Almost eight minutes have passed. The second guy who will team up with me finishes in that group; he had a strong sprint finish. Five more minutes and I can see Aaron crossing the line alone, almost exhausted. He falls and two medical nurses rush over him. He has a sad facial expression –I can almost see him crying but can't hear anything. He sips some drink the nurses give him and he immediately recovers some energy, and he drinks more.

I start to change my running shoes and get rid of some of the dry salt accumulated over my arms because of the sweat. I take off my vest with the number still pinned on, 201. I will remember this one for a long time.

A race organizer approaches me and hands over an envelope that reads: "Mexican national team member invitation form"; for me this is the prize but Gustavo ironically says: no prize money, eh? I see his father's van and we walk together, as we get closer I can see our massage therapist already working on one of our elite runners. Towels are in hand to clean up our faces and get a fresh drink and some bananas.

I look back at his father and he says that today is a very special day for the club: Alcala finishes second overall and we got Lazo and Gustavo finishing on the top 20. "The best the club has ever done", I say. But then out of nothing he adds: but we also have a new female club member winning the race. At that point the

Blond girl comes out from the back of his car. What shall I do, clap? No, this would mean that I don't mind she outsprinted me. She smiles and I just think that all those losers who congratulate their opponents are not real sport contenders.

The Blond hands over a flower from her bouquet to Gustavo and another one to me; I feel a sense of superiority on this act but I accept it and she immediately gets closer and says: "you pushed too early." Who does she think she is? This is the first time I see her. "You should have either steadily pushed away two or three kilometres before or waited until the last few metres, I only had to wait until you pushed and then just followed you and passed you". You picked the wrong moment to sprint you idiot!

I'm circled now by Gustavo and the club runners making jokes about the Blond beating me and all of a sudden she is besides me. We look at each other; all eyes are on us. How would a great champion react to this pressure? Get a good excuse –I think. But no, let's go with the truth.

"Did you have anything left on your legs for those final metres?" I ask.

"No, but I was carried away by your sprint; if you had pushed more, I probably could not have followed you.

I admire her honest answer, the bright girl strikes again. "I thought you were far back" I admit, maybe I should've just kept pushing.

Half an hour since we finished and Evert is just showing up. He comes straight to me and says: "excellent". That is all he says. He has never been a man of many words but I don't remember him saying this word for a long time.

Every few minutes more runners finish, and the cheering gets louder and louder. I get into the van and think of the nice bath that's waiting for me at the hotel; still a lot of traffic ahead to get us out of here. My mind is somewhere else, thinking of what I think when I run. Alcala is sitting at the front and turns his head to ask: 'so now you, Lazo, need to start thinking about the next marathon' and he turns forward as a good patron would do. I'm left with the Blond girl sitting beside me with her eyes closed.

She may also be thinking of that last moment, around the park, with the shaded trees in the central area of Torreon where the great LALA marathon is held; town of dryness and solitude, where only the ravens and the zopilotes are happy with the weather.